THE WALKING STICK

BY MAXINE TROTTIER
ILLUSTRATED BY ANNOUCHKA GRAVEL GALOUCHKO

Stoddart
Kids
TORONTO • NEW YORK

for Bern
— M. T.

for those who have the courage to walk a different path,
to those who find strength in walking alone,
to independent spirits, but especially for Sacha,
who was with me throughout this work,
and born when it was finished — a beautiful masterpiece
— A. G. G.

Text copyright © 1998 by Maxine Trottier
Illustrations copyright © 1998 by Annouchka Gravel Galouchko

With thanks to Dien Tran for his wisdom—M.T.

We acknowledge the Canada Council for the Arts and the
Ontario Arts Council for their support of our publishing program.

Published in Canada in 1998 by
Stoddart Kids,
a division of Stoddart Publishing Co. Limited
34 Lesmill Road
Toronto, Canada M3B 2T6
Tel (416) 445-3333 Fax (416) 445-5967
E-mail Customer.Service@ccmailgw.genpub.com

Distributed in Canada by
General Distribution Services
30 Lesmill Road
Toronto, Canada M3B 2T6
Tel (416) 445-3333 Fax (416) 445-5967
E-mail Customer.Service@ccmailgw.genpub.com

Published in the United States in 1999 by
Stoddart Kids
a division of Stoddart Publishing Co. Limited
180 Varick Street, 9th Floor
New York, New York 14207
Toll free 1-800-805-1083
E-mail gdsinc@genpub.com

Distributed in the United States by
General Distribution Services
85 River Rock Drive, Suite 202
Buffalo, New York 14207
Toll free 1-800-805-1083
E-mail gdsinc@genpub.com

Canadian Cataloguing in Publication Data

Trottier, Maxine
Walking stick

ISBN 0-7737-3101-6

I. Galouchko, Annouchka. II. Title.

PS8589.R685W34 1998   jC813'.54   C98-930494-9
PZ7.T66Wa 1998

Printed and bound in Hong Kong, China by
Book Art Inc., Toronto

When Van was a boy wandering the forest of Vietnam, he found the stick. It had fallen from a great teak tree. That tree had grown near the Buddhist temple for hundreds of years. In the monsoon rains a branch or two might break off. But the tree stood strong and silent, weathering the changes that swept across the country.

Van took the stick into the temple where the monks lived. With their shaved heads made shiny by the damp heat, and their soft robes wrapped around them, the monks prayed and chanted. One of those monks was Van's uncle.

"He is not like other boys," his uncle often thought. "He must always see just what is beyond the next hill."

Together they cleaned and polished the stick. Van's uncle fitted a brass cover over its tip. When they finished, the walking stick glowed with the quiet life of the teak forests of Vietnam.

"You found this stick near the temple under the shadow of Buddha," said Van's uncle. "He will watch over you no matter where you go, and bring you safely home."

Van treasured the walking stick. He used it every day as he went from his home to the rice fields or market.

Each night he polished the stick until the teak and brass softly
shone.

The years passed. Van married, and in time he and his wife Mai had a daughter. They named her Lan. When festivals came, the family would go to the temple. The little girl loved the smell of incense and the echoing drone of the monks' chanting. Van's uncle still lived there. Now he was a very old man, small and wrinkled.

"Ah, Van," he would say, his face lit with a toothless smile, "I see you still have the walking stick."

From monsoon to harvest it was a good life, rich with rice and the wind in the palms. But the wind can blow in many things.

When war came too close and Van heard the roar of jets in the night, he picked up the walking stick. He sat on his heels, thinking, until the sun rose. "We will walk," he said to his family. And that is what they did.

At first they had a cart that their water buffalo pulled. Then when they had to, they went on without it, carrying their few possessions. They crept through the forests full of nervous birds and small, bright-eyed monkeys. Bombed rice paddies and smoking villages crushed in the mud — all these things they saw. Van held his walking stick tightly and led his family from Vietnam.

They came to the sea. There Van spent almost all of his money for passage on a ship to cross the ocean. Grey waves rolled and carried the rusty vessel to the east, away from the sound of temple chimes and the bustling markets of Vietnam. Van would stand at the ship's rail, the stick in his hand. At night while Mai and Lan were asleep, he walked the deck under the cold unseeing stars and wept.

The new country █████████████████ █ one spoke
Vietnamese. The ████████████████████ ad of bicycles.
Still, the war had ███████████████████ rs passed in
peace.

One day a young ████████████████████ on his daughter.
He had very yello ████████████████████ eyes were full of
love when they lo ████████████████████ ater there was a
baby. They named ████████

daughter got married

Each afternoon Van walked with his granddaughter down the streets of their neighborhood. The brass tip of the stick tapped against the sidewalk. Van told stories of the land he had left behind. He talked about his uncle and the temple with its cool, mossy walls and calm Buddha.

Deep inside Lynn, the stories took hold like tiny vines. Their tendrils wound 'round her heart as the walking stick tap, tap, tapped.

Then, Lynn was grown and Van was a very old man. She had the startling blue eyes of her father and her mother's silky, straight, black hair. Within her were all the stories she had ever heard.

"I am going on a long walk, Grandfather," she told Van one evening. For a moment the fragrance of incense drifted in the air and he heard the soft chanting of monks.

"This does not surprise me," said Van. "You have always seemed like a child who must see beyond the next hill." And he gave the walking stick to his granddaughter.

That spring when Lynn was finished school, she sailed across the ocean. Each night the sun set upon the country she called home. Each day it rose over the land her family had fled so long ago. In time the crossing ended and the river waters welcomed her.

It was morning when Lynn stepped onto the soil of Vietnam. She started out, tapping the ground with the walking stick. Chickens and fat bellied pigs stood outside the houses and watched as she passed. After a very long time, she came to a temple.

Soft moss clung to its walls and all around the jungle sang. Nearby
was a huge teak tree. Into the temple she went, the walking stick
held in her hands, its brass voice finally silent.

There stood the Buddha, still and smiling. At his feet lay offerings of flowers and food, and in the peaceful air a memory of sweet incense drifted.

Lynn slowly ran her hand along Van's walking stick. She said a prayer of thanks to the god who had watched over such a long journey and those who had made it. Lynn placed the stick at the foot of the Buddha. Then she turned and began her walk home.